SNAP!

BY JANET A. HOLMES
ILLUSTRATED BY DANIELLA GERMAIN

LITTLE HARE
www.littleharebooks.com

To Michael and Sophia Rakic — JAH

To Ruby, for always being
by my side while I work — DG

Little Hare Books
an imprint of
Hardie Grant Egmont
Ground Floor, Building 1, 658 Church Street
Richmond, Victoria 3121, Australia

www.littleharebooks.com

First published 2013

Cataloguing-in-Publication details are available from the
National Library of Australia

978 1 921 714 993 (hbk.)

Designed by Vida & Luke Kelly
Produced by Pica Digital, Singapore
Printed through Phoenix Offset
Printed in Shen Zhen, Guangdong Province, China, October 2012

5 4 3 2 1

*The illustrations in this book were created with watercolour
and ink combined with collage.*

It was the big day.
I got up and hid
under the bed.

"I don't want to go," I said.

"There are monsters there."

I put on my jeans and my T-shirt,
my socks and my shoes.

And my crocodile face.

"Snap!"

I said when I got in the car.

"Snap!"

I said when they left me there.

"Snap!" I said when they showed me toys.

"Snap!" I said when they gave me cake.

"Snap!"

I said when they read me a story.

There were monsters
everywhere.

I ran outside.

The monsters followed.

I crawled to a place
at the end of the yard
and sat on a log
all alone.

The monsters stayed far away.

Except one.
A little monster.
Smaller than me.

I snapped at her with
my crocodile mouth.

But she did not go away.
She sat at the other end of the log.

"Go away," I snapped.

"This is my log."

"No, it isn't. I can sit here if I want," she said.

She took some crayons and paper out of her pocket
and started drawing.

I didn't look
for a long time.

Then I moved a bit closer.
She kept drawing.

I moved a bit closer.
She didn't say anything, but she kept drawing.

I moved right next to her.

"What's that?"
I said.

"It's a monkey face,"
she said.

The monkey face was smiling.

I liked that face.

I wanted that face.

"Can I try it on?"
I said.

"If you want,"
she said.

I put on the monkey face.
It fitted perfectly.

"You look like a friendly monkey," she said.

"Do you want to play?"
I asked.

We rode on bikes.

We painted pictures.

And then it was time
to go home.

I took off my shoes and my socks,
my jeans and my T-shirt,
and put on my pyjamas.

Then I climbed into bed.